A FIGHTING CHANCE

Also available:
The Magic Begins
Potions and Poison

Coming soon:
Sword and Sorcery

For older readers:
The Dragon's Call
Valiant
The Mark of Nimueh

Coming soon for older readers:
The Poisoned Chalice

A FIGHTING CHANCE

BANTAM BOOKS

MERLIN: A FIGHTING CHANCE
A BANTAM BOOK 978 0 553 82501 5

First published in Great Britain by Bantam,
an imprint of Random House Children's Books
A Random House Group Company

This edition published 2009

1 3 5 7 9 10 8 6 4 2

The Random House Group Limited supports the Forest Stewardship Council
(FSC), the leading international forest certification organization. All our titles that
are printed on Greenpeace-approved FSC-certified paper carry the FSC logo. Our
paper procurement policy can be found at www.rbooks.co.uk/environment.

Typeset in 16/22 Bembo Schlbk by Falcon Oast Graphic Art Ltd.

Bantam Books are published by Random House Children's Books,
61–63 Uxbridge Road, London W5 5SA

www.**kids**at**randomhouse**.co.uk
www.**rbooks**.co.uk

Addresses for companies within The Random House Group Limited can be found
at: www.randomhouse.co.uk/offices.htm

THE RANDOM HOUSE GROUP Limited Reg. No. 954009

A CIP catalogue record for this book is available from the British Library.

Printed in the UK by CPI Bookmarque, Croydon, CR0 4TD

With grateful thanks to
Johnny Capps, Julian Murphy,
Polly Buckle, Rachel Knight, Sarah Dollard,
Jamie Munro, Pindy O'Brien, Filiz Tosun,
Anna Nettle and Rebecca Morris

CONTENTS

CHAPTER ONE
PERIL IN CAMELOT

A shaft of sunlight broke through the trees and illuminated a patch of toadstools. Merlin made his way over and began to pick them one by one and put them in his knapsack. He was wary, knowing that some of them could be very poisonous. However, Gaius – who knew all about herbs and plants and things like that because he was Camelot's court physician – had asked him to collect them and assured him he would come to no harm if he was careful. After all, Merlin dealt with dangerous things almost every day. What were a few toadstools compared to Knight Valiant and his deadly shield, or the plague brought by the terrible Afanc?

The thing was, as well as being Gaius' dogsbody, Merlin was also manservant to Prince Arthur, heir to the throne of Camelot. And as well as being Arthur's manservant, he was also a warlock – possibly the greatest warlock ever – who was destined to protect Arthur and help him become king. That involved facing all sorts of dangers, many of them magical. And the greatest danger he faced was someone discovering his secret, because sorcery was forbidden in Camelot on pain of death. Only Gaius knew of Merlin's true nature; if anyone else found out, the boy would almost certainly be executed.

So he wouldn't worry about the toadstools,

he would just enjoy his relaxing walk in the woods and be thankful that no one and nothing was trying to kill him for once.

Merlin's enjoyment was short-lived. Suddenly a piercing screech filled the air. The boy looked up and was terrified to see a huge beast galloping towards him through the trees. At the front it was like an eagle, although a hundred times the size, with a wickedly hooked beak, sharp claws and vast wings. Its back half was like a lion's, with powerfully muscled legs. As it advanced, its cruel eyes were fixed on Merlin, and there was no doubt that it was looking for prey.

Merlin dropped his knapsack and fled. He was running as fast as he possibly could, but the creature was gaining on him easily. He turned to see how near it was – and lost his balance, falling heavily to the ground. Terrified, he rolled over, trying to get up again, but the beast had reached him and was rearing above him, its talons and beak ready to strike. Merlin closed his eyes . . .

But death didn't come. Instead he heard a shout from nearby: he opened his eyes to see a man swinging bravely at the monster with a sword.

To Merlin's horror, the sword shattered as it hit the creature's belly. 'Run! Run!' the man yelled, darting towards Merlin and dragging him up by one arm. The two of them took to their heels, the beast following close behind. They entered a clearing and dived behind a fallen tree – and to Merlin's immense relief and delight, the monster spread its wings

RUN!

and soared into the air.

He turned to the man beside him. 'You saved my life!'

His companion was gasping for breath after their flight, but managed a nod.

Merlin offered his hand. 'I'm Merlin.'

'Lancelot,' came the reply. The man took Merlin's hand – but his grip suddenly loosened. His arm flopped limply to his side, and his head fell back. Merlin was horrified to see that blood was seeping through the man's shirt.

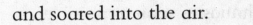

It was evening by the time Merlin reached Camelot. Although he was quite strong, moving the unconscious warrior had proved too big a job for him alone, and he'd had to run to the nearest village for help. Every minute's delay had worried him – he knew he had to get Lancelot into Gaius' expert hands as soon as possible.

Now the man lay on a bed in Gaius' candlelit chambers as the doctor finished examining the injury. It was clear that a claw had slashed across Lancelot's stomach, but Gaius didn't look too worried. 'The wound itself is superficial,' he said. 'The fever will pass and he should be fine by the morning.'

Merlin breathed a sigh of relief. Lancelot had saved him from a terrible fate; thank goodness he wasn't badly hurt as a consequence.

But where had that monster come from? What was it? And where had it gone . . . ?

★

The answer to the last question was only too obvious the next morning when Prince Arthur and his father, King Uther, rode to the top of a hill and surveyed the village below – or rather, what was left of the village. Smoke and flames rose from the ruins.

'The villagers say the monster has wings,' Arthur said. 'We found no tracks, so it must be true. And ...' He trailed off, finding it hard to speak the words.

'What?' Uther demanded.

'It took no livestock. Only people. Whatever it is – it has a taste for human flesh.'

The king's face was hard. 'Post sentries at all the outlying villages. Put the lookouts on full alert. If this thing should make for Camelot we must be ready.'

Gaius' diagnosis had turned out to be correct. By morning, Lancelot seemed fully recovered, and Merlin took an immediate liking to the soft-spoken warrior when he finally got to meet him properly.

Now Lancelot was gazing out of the window, dreamily regarding the city below. 'Ever since I was a child I dreamed of coming here,' he said. 'It is my life's ambition to join the Knights of Camelot.'

Merlin had no particularly romantic view of the knights – their most recent battle had been a food fight during a celebratory feast – it had taken him hours to clean all the custard off Arthur's clothes. He raised his eyebrows in surprise.

WHATEVER IT IS – IT HAS A TASTE FOR HUMAN FLESH.

Lancelot misinterpreted the look. 'I know what you're thinking. I expect too much. After all, who am I? They have their pick of the best and bravest in the land.'

Merlin finally managed to get a word in. 'Lancelot – they're going to love you! I've seen you in action. In fact, you know what I'm going to do? I'm going to talk to Arthur right now.'

'You *know* Arthur?' Lancelot was amazed.

'Oh yes,' said Merlin.

CHAPTER TWO
A BITTER BLOW

Arthur was at the training ground, facing a would-be knight.

'Right, you jumped-up dung beetle, this is it,' he announced. 'Your final test. Pass this, and you're a Knight of Camelot. Fail – and you're no one. You face the most feared of all foes, the ultimate killing machine.' He smiled. 'You face me.' Arthur's opponent seemed unmoved as the prince carried on. 'Your challenge is to last one minute in free combat. Grimond, second son of Wessex – your time starts now.'

Arthur drew his sword as another knight turned over a minute-glass. Grimond moved forward, waving his two swords with arrogant confidence. With a yell, he slashed at the prince – and Arthur ducked under the blade to plant a knee in the knight's stomach and a fist under his chin. Grimond toppled backwards and the prince moved away, shaking his head in disgust over the fallen warrior.

Merlin, watching, couldn't believe his luck. What a perfect time to present Arthur with a great fighter like Lancelot! He was certain his friend could easily pass the prince's test.

'How am I meant to defend Camelot with rubbish like that?' Arthur demanded as Merlin hurried up, although he obviously didn't expect his servant to answer.

But it was exactly the opportunity Merlin needed! 'I think I might be able to help,' he said.

'You?' Arthur sounded sceptical, to say the least. 'You haven't the faintest idea what it takes to be a knight. Courage, fortitude, discipline . . .'

'No, of course I don't have that,' said Merlin, who had learned not to be offended by Arthur's dismissive attitude towards him. 'But I do know someone who has.'

'Yeah?'

Merlin nodded. 'He saved my life.'

The prince laughed. 'That's blown it for starters.'

'No, no, he's really good . . .'

But Arthur still wasn't taking him seriously. 'That's great, Merlin, I'm sure he's terrific. But you forget the First Code of Camelot. Only those of noble blood can serve as knights. So unless your friend is a nobleman . . .'

No! Merlin wanted to shout in frustration. But then . . . well, Lancelot *might* be a nobleman for all he knew. The tall, dignified young man certainly seemed more noble than a lot of those custard-throwing knights that Arthur hung around with. 'He *is* a nobleman!' the warlock said hurriedly.

Arthur seemed surprised. Well, he probably didn't expect a servant to have aristocratic friends. 'Is he?' the prince said. 'Very well. Bring him to the training ground tomorrow.'

Merlin grinned his thanks and turned to

MAKE SURE HE BRINGS HIS SEAL OF NOBILITY.

leave. But the smile faded as Arthur added, 'And make sure he brings his seal of nobility.'

Merlin decided he wouldn't worry about that just now. He made his way back to Gaius' chambers, where Lancelot was waiting for him. The man came rushing up, his face anxious. 'Did you speak to Arthur?'

'Yeah,' Merlin replied.

'And?'

He'd give him the good news first. They could deal with any problems later. 'And . . . he said he'd like to meet you!'

Lancelot beamed. He grasped both of Merlin's hands in gratitude. 'Oh, thank you, thank you!'

Merlin tried to look modest, as if it was no big deal to have the ear of the prince of the realm. 'No problem. Really. It was nothing.' And then, hoping against hope that the answer was yes, he added casually, 'You're not a nobleman by any chance, are you?'

'A *nobleman*?' Lancelot laughed in surprise. 'Good Lord, no. Why do you ask?'

Merlin waved a hand dismissively. But Gaius had been listening to the conversation and came over to join them. 'The First Code of Camelot states that only those of noble blood can serve as a knight,' the doctor said. 'Uther created the knights to protect this kingdom from those who wished to destroy it. He knew that he'd have to trust each of them with his life. So he chose them from the noble

families that had sworn allegiance to him.'
Lancelot's face grew longer and longer as
he listened to Gaius' words. 'Thus the First
Code of Camelot was born. And ever
since that day only the sons of the noble
families have served as knights.'

It just wasn't fair! Merlin looked at
Lancelot, seeing how he tried to take even
this devastating blow with dignity, and
felt terrible. He'd raised his friend's hopes
for nothing.

Lancelot's dream was over. That dream had
been his life for so many years now and
the disappointment was almost unbearable.
He felt as if he were no longer a person,
just a collection of bones and flesh that
kept on breathing and moving but had no
purpose. Yet he had to go on, out of respect
for those who were no longer living.

And he had much to be thankful for, he

could not deny that. The kindness of the physician, Gaius, who had treated his injuries. The friendship of Merlin, who had brought him back from the forest and had even spoken to the great Prince Arthur on his behalf. They had given him food and shelter too. To wallow in misery in the face of such generosity would be the height of rudeness.

But misery threatened to overwhelm him later that night as his new friend Merlin spoke to him, bringing back such terrible memories.

'Why do you want to be a knight so much?' the boy asked as they sat together in Merlin's small room.

It was a moment before Lancelot answered. He gazed over Merlin's shoulder, looking into the past. This must not overwhelm him. Telling the story was just words. Finally he said quietly, 'When I was a boy my village was attacked by raiders from the northern plains. The people were slaughtered where they stood. My father, my mother . . . everyone. I alone escaped. I vowed that day that never again would I be helpless in the face of tyranny. I made swordcraft my life. Every waking hour since that day I devoted to the art of combat. And when I was ready, I set forth for Camelot.' He sighed, remembering the hope in his heart as he began his long journey. Hope that was now gone. 'And now it seems my journey ends. Everything I've fought for, wasted.'

Merlin was silent for a second, and then said softly, 'I give you my word: whatever it takes – I will make this right.'

Lancelot smiled sadly. He knew that the youth meant every word he said. But he also knew that this was a promise that could not be kept.

CHAPTER THREE
ONE SMALL LIE

The keeper of the Hall of Records was keeping a close eye on Merlin as the boy browsed along the shelves. Merlin gave the old man a reassuring look, trying to convince him that nothing at all suspicious was going on. 'Just doing some homework,' he explained.

He pulled from a shelf a large, dusty volume entitled *Ancient Families of Britain*. Overnight, he'd had the most brilliant brainwave.

It had seemed so desperately unfair that
Lancelot wouldn't even get a trial for the
knights – in Merlin's eyes, he had a lot
more right to have a go than the noble
'rubbish' that Arthur had been moaning
about. But what if Lancelot did get a
trial? He'd pass it with flying colours,
Merlin had no doubt about that. Then
Arthur would realize what a brilliant
fighter he was, what a great guy, and the
prince would surely let him be a knight,
noble or not! If Lancelot could only turn
up to the training ground tomorrow with
a seal of nobility, he was as good as a
knight already.

So here was Merlin, searching through
the records for a suitable noble seal.

He paused at the colourful crest for
Richard, fourth son of Lord Eldred of
Northumbria. Well, Northumbria was a
long way away, and there were none of

Eldred's relations in Camelot as far as he knew. That was the one!

Quickly checking that the records keeper was busy at the other end of the room, Merlin drew a blank parchment from inside his jacket and laid it out by the book. He began to incant a spell, and slowly, very slowly, the seal began to take shape on the parchment.

He glanced over his shoulder again. To his horror, the old man had got up from his desk and was walking towards Merlin! 'Come on, come on!' the boy muttered urgently as the words *Lancelot, fifth son of* . . . appeared.

Closer and closer came the records keeper. As the final 'a' of *Northumbria* appeared, Merlin snatched up the parchment, shoving it inside his jacket just as the old man appeared by his side. With a smile, Merlin thrust the book into the man's hands. 'Real

page-turner,' he said, and left with a spring
in his step.

Lancelot looked up as Merlin bounded into
Gaius' chambers with a huge smile on his
face. The youth waved a scroll at him as if
he were a dog with an especially excellent
bone.

'What's that?' Lancelot asked.

'This is your seal of nobility,' Merlin replied. He unrolled the parchment with a flourish. 'Ladies and gentlemen, I give you Lancelot, fifth son of Lord Eldred of Northumbria!'

Lancelot smiled at Merlin's excitement, but shook his head. 'No, Merlin, no.'

'So you don't want to be a knight, then?'

Lancelot almost shouted, 'Of course I do!' Then he pulled himself up, ashamed. Merlin was trying to help, and he had certainly not intended an insult; he was just trying to get Lancelot to go along with his plan. But Lancelot could not do so. He could not be party to a lie. Acting with such dishonour would only prove his unworthiness.

He wanted to explain this to Merlin, but could not find the words. 'It's against everything the knights stand for,' he tried. 'The rules ...'

'We're not breaking the rules,' Merlin

assured him. 'We're bending them. You get your foot in the door ... After that, you'll be judged on your merit alone. If you succeed – if they make you a knight – it'll be because you've earned it, noble or not.'

Lancelot was almost persuaded. Such a small lie ... what harm could it cause? Merlin was right, he would succeed – or fail – on his own merits, not because of any piece of paper.

But a man who opened his heart to a small lie would perhaps then open his heart to a bigger one, and when would it ever stop? He must refuse.

Then Merlin said, '*I* can't change the way things are done round here. But you can. If you let me help you ...'

The words, the look on the boy's face, touched Lancelot deeply. Merlin wanted this so much. He was desperate to help

Lancelot, and the warrior knew why – because he had saved him from the monster in the forest. For Lancelot, the debt had already been settled with kindness and friendship, but he knew that Merlin would not accept that. A man of honour himself, he realized that this was a matter of honour for the boy.

So Lancelot had a choice – the small lie, or a great insult to a friend.

The lie was so small. It would hurt no one. It would make Merlin happy.

And on top of that, it might lead to Lancelot's dream coming true. It could give him a chance to stand up against tyranny and evil. Surely that would all outweigh just one small lie . . .

Yet even as he agreed to Merlin's plan, Lancelot still felt dead inside. His hope had been destroyed once, and he remained empty, hollow. He barely listened as Merlin outlined his plan to obtain suitable clothes for a nobleman – something about a seamstress friend who would be happy to sew them.

The two of them went into the town, and Merlin knocked on the door of the house that this seamstress shared with her black-smith father. A few moments later, a young woman opened the door.

And suddenly Lancelot had a reason for living again.

Merlin knew that Gwen was an excellent seamstress, and what was more, he knew he could count on her. She was maid to the Lady Morgana, King Uther's ward, and was probably Merlin's best friend in Camelot. She was sweet and kind and always ready to help anyone in need – and sure enough, she immediately agreed to come to their aid. Fetching a tape, she began to measure Lancelot for a new outfit.

'This is very kind of you, er ...' As Lancelot stuttered his thanks, Merlin realized that he hadn't actually introduced the two to each other; he'd been too busy telling Gwen about his plan to get Lancelot made a knight. He also realized that these were the first words that Lancelot had spoken since they'd arrived, and that the man sounded strangely shy and nervous.

'Gwen,' Gwen told him. 'Short for Guinevere.'

'Then thank you, Guinevere.' Lancelot seemed unable to take his eyes off her.

Gwen smiled awkwardly. 'Oh, don't thank me, thank Merlin. Merlin would do anything for anyone. I think it's great that he's got you this chance. We need men like you.'

'You do?' Lancelot replied softly.

'Well, not me personally,' the girl said hastily. 'But, you know, Camelot. Camelot needs knights. Not just Arthur and his kind but ordinary people like you and me.'

Lancelot stared deeply into her eyes. 'Well, I am not yet a knight, my lady.'

'And I'm not a lady.' She gave an embarrassed laugh and looked away. 'OK, we're done. I should have these ready in no time. It's nice to meet you, Lancelot.' She held out a hand, but instead of shaking it he seized it and raised it to his lips.

'She seems lovely,' Lancelot said as they walked back to the castle.

'Oh, yeah, she is,' Merlin told him.

Lancelot seemed almost embarrassed as he asked, 'Are you two . . . you know?'

The warlock laughed. 'No. No . . . just friends.' He shot a sly glance at Lancelot, who seemed to be thinking very deeply about something – and Merlin was fairly sure he knew what. Or rather, whom . . .

CHAPTER FOUR
LANCELOT'S CHANCE

Gwen was as good as her word. Only hours later, Lancelot stood at the edge of the training ground wearing a fine orange tabard bearing the Northumbrian crest.

'Well, you certainly look the part,' Merlin said.

Gwen smiled. 'Doesn't he just.'

'I don't feel it,' Lancelot told them. He took a deep, nervous breath, then made his way over to Arthur.

The prince looked up from a rack of swords. 'Yes?'

'Lancelot – fifth son of Lord Eldred of Northumbria.'

Arthur didn't seem particularly interested. 'Lance-a-lot. Oh yes, my servant mentioned you. Got your seal?'

Lancelot held out Merlin's faked scroll, bowing respectfully to the prince. As he straightened up, Arthur's fist shot out, striking him on the chin. Gwen and Merlin gasped in horror to see Lancelot stumbling backwards, falling to the ground.

'Sluggish reactions. On a battlefield you'd be dead by now.' Arthur turned away contemptuously. 'Come back when you're ready.'

Lancelot rose to his feet, his hand on the hilt of his sword. 'I'm ready now, sire.'

'You are, are you?' said Arthur.

Merlin looked anxiously at the prince's

face. Arthur didn't take kindly to anyone answering him back. But he spotted the ghost of a smile. That was another thing about Arthur – he respected determination and self-belief.

'Fine,' said the prince. 'You can start by cleaning out the stables.'

Lancelot looked devastated as he took his hand from his sword. A few nearby knights laughed scornfully. But Merlin beamed, giving the would-be warrior a jaunty thumbs-up. He knew that Lancelot was going to be all right.

Whether Lancelot thought of it in quite the same way was hard to tell, because when he staggered into Gaius' chambers that evening, exhausted and filthy, he barely paused to grunt a greeting before heading off again, probably towards a bath.

Gaius looked questioningly at Merlin.

The warlock gave him a sheepish smile. He'd avoided mentioning any of the day's events, knowing that Gaius would not be pleased – to put it mildly. 'Er ... he found work at the stables,' he tried.

'I see! And the truth, before I lose my temper?' the physician demanded.

Merlin decided that trying to bluff any further would be rather dangerous. 'He's, er, trying out for the knights.'

Of course, Gaius lost his temper anyway. 'The First Code of Camelot has never been broken for any man. What have you done, Merlin?'

'OK, I bent the rules a little,' he admitted. 'But the rules are wrong, they're unfair—'

It seemed that Gaius was in no mood to listen to Merlin's justifications. If anything, they made him more angry. 'You bent the rules – using magic?'

Now they were on really sticky ground.

Gaius had very definite views on the use of magic: it was to be used only in the direst of emergencies – usually meaning if Arthur's life was at risk – and even then only if no other option was available.

'It was more of a trick than actual magic . . .' Merlin tried, but even to his own ears the words didn't sound convincing.

Gaius was furious. 'Your magic is not a *toy*! It is not yours to use and abuse as you see fit!'

The thing was, Merlin knew that. And he'd been trying hard not to take sorcery for granted, not to use it for every little chore and task that presented itself, but sometimes something came along that was really important to him. He had to make Gaius understand that this was no trivial matter – this was more than the right thing to do; it was the *only* thing to do.

'I owe Lancelot my life!' he cried,

remembering the beast rearing over him, the certainty of death, the unspeakable joy and relief when the young warrior had appeared and saved him. 'I am paying for that debt the only way I can: by giving him the opportunity he deserves. If you want to punish me for it – go ahead.' And filled with righteous anger, Merlin stormed off to his room.

The next day Arthur set Lancelot to work again – sharpening swords, a vast pile of them. The prince had to fight to hide a smile as he came round a corner and spotted the man sweating at his task. Merlin would have been interested to know that he'd been quite right about Arthur: the prince did like to see determination, a refusal to give in. He also respected hard work. But what Merlin didn't know was that Arthur had sensed something in this man. He might have acted dismissively, but he'd realized instinctively that he had a true warrior before him. Lancelot probably thought that he was being given these difficult and dirty jobs as a punishment for failing Arthur's first test; in reality they were part of the test – he was proving to the prince that he had the necessary dedication.

Arthur picked up a broom and threw it at the seated man. He was pleased to note that Lancelot's hand immediately sprang out and grabbed it, even though he hadn't even been looking in the prince's direction.

'Not bad,' Arthur commented.

Lancelot looked at the broom. 'Would you like me to sweep the guardhouse again, sire?'

'Well, it certainly needs sweeping,' Arthur said – and then added, looking forward to the effect his words had, 'But first I'd like you to kill me.' Lancelot stared in astonishment, but the prince could see the words appealed to him. 'Come on. Don't pretend you don't want to. If I were you I'd want to!' He picked up a broomstick and took up a fighting stance.

Lancelot stood up. He knocked the head off his own broom – and launched himself at Arthur.

The battle was ferocious. Neither man held back. Arthur was astonished, and delighted, by Lancelot's skill. For the first time in many years he felt he was fighting an equal – or at least, a man who could be his equal when properly trained.

Of course, in the end the prince's experience won through, and he finally landed a decisive blow to Lancelot's stomach. As his opponent gasped and stepped back, Arthur grinned. 'Congratulations, Lancelot. You just made basic training.'

He turned away, thoroughly pleased. There was no question – this man was going to be a huge asset to Camelot. But his joy didn't last long. As he walked away from Lancelot, a bell began to toll. It was the warning bell. Disaster was coming to the city.

CHAPTER FIVE
A TESTING TIME

Merlin had barely spoken to Gaius since their argument the day before, but all animosity was forgotten as the warning bell sounded. They looked at each other in horror and then ran outside as fast as they could to see what was happening; to see if they could help in any way.

Merlin would never forget the sight that awaited them. A line of people stumbling into the city, tattered and bleeding, sobbing and wailing. It was almost overwhelming — with so many injured surrounding them, who did they treat first? But Gaius set to work calmly and methodically, and Merlin did his best to follow the doctor's lead.

The patients began to tell their story. Some sounded as though they expected not to be believed, but Merlin had no trouble at all in accepting their word.

Lancelot hurried over. 'What happened to these people?' he cried.

Gaius looked up. 'Their village was attacked. By a winged monster.'

Lancelot and Merlin exchanged a glance. They knew exactly what these villagers had faced. The only

surprise was that so many had lived to tell the tale.

THEIR VILLAGE WAS ATTACKED. BY A WINGED MONSTER.

Having heard the villagers' story, Lancelot hurried off. The knights would surely be intending to challenge this creature, and he wanted to be with them when they did. He found them assembled at the training ground, where Arthur was addressing them all. 'The beast attacked Greensward, then Willowdale. It's travelling south. Towards us. Towards Camelot. We must be ready to fight it. It's fast and agile, but big enough to hit, and to hit hard. Starting today, all training routines will concentrate on an attack strategy. We don't have much time. Dismissed.'

The knights bowed, then began to file away. Lancelot went over to the prince. 'Is there anything I can do, sire?' He took a deep breath. 'It's just . . . I know that in the event of battle only a knight may serve . . .'

Arthur nodded. 'That's correct, Lancelot – and you are not yet a knight.'

Lancelot bowed his head. He was not surprised that his offer of help was being dismissed.

But Arthur continued: 'Which is why I'm bringing your test forward. You'll face me in the morning.'

As the prince walked off, Lancelot felt exhilarated. This was it! His dream was so near! The morning could not come soon enough.

★

Once again, Merlin and Gwen stood at the edge of the training ground. Once again, Arthur and Lancelot stood before them. But the atmosphere was very different this time. Even the watching knights seemed tense – but then they, better than anyone, knew just how important this test was.

The prince did nothing to ease the tension. His face was stern as he spoke. He addressed all those present, although his words were aimed at Lancelot. 'The final challenge. Succeed, and you join the elite. Fail – and your journey ends here.' He pulled his helmet over his head, readying himself for battle. 'Lancelot, fifth son of Lord Eldred of Northumbria, your time starts now.'

On Arthur's word, a knight turned over the minute-glass. As the sand began to run through, the two warriors drew their swords and advanced on each other.

The fighting was furious. Merlin thought

he'd never seen such an intense contest. Gwen grabbed his tunic as the tension mounted to unbearable levels – then quickly released it with an apology. It seemed that the fight had been going on for ever – but no, the grains of sand still continued their steady voyage to the bottom of the glass.

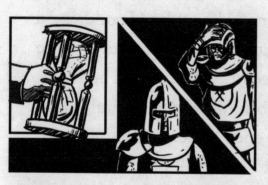

And then, horrifyingly, it all appeared to be over. Lancelot held out his sword to parry Arthur's blow – and the prince's other arm swept in for a punch. Arthur's challenger lay senseless on the ground.

Gwen gasped in shock. Merlin couldn't believe it. Surely it couldn't end here? Surely that single blow couldn't have destroyed all Lancelot's hopes and dreams?

Arthur stuck his sword in the ground and walked over to his fallen opponent. 'Shame,' he said as he bent down to remove Lancelot's colours.

And then – Merlin could barely follow what was going on, it happened so fast – the seemingly unconscious man had grabbed hold of Arthur's outstretched arm, kicked his legs from under him; and now here was Lancelot standing with his sword pointed straight at the fallen, helpless prince. 'Do you submit, sire?' he demanded.

Gwen stifled a laugh of delight – but Merlin didn't dare smile. Knights were coming forward to drag Lancelot away. The sands of time had run out – but would Arthur consider that Lancelot had lasted a minute in combat; would he appreciate that the man had echoed his own earlier tactic to defeat him – or would he consider the other's actions a deadly insult and humiliation?

He feared he knew the answer. Arthur's face radiated fury. 'On your knees!' he barked, rising to his feet. He stormed towards Lancelot. The knights forced the young man to the ground, and Arthur's sword pointed towards him . . .

CHAPTER SIX
DISCOVERY

Lancelot knelt and a sword pointed towards him . . .

But it was later that day, he was in the great hall, and the sword belonged to King Uther.

Uther held the sword above Lancelot, resting it first on one shoulder then the other, and smiled a rare smile. 'Arise, Sir Lancelot, Knight of Camelot!'

There was huge applause from everyone – Arthur and his knights, Gaius and Gwen, the courtiers and nobles – but Merlin applauded hardest of all. He could barely contain his delight. His plan had worked brilliantly; better than he'd dared to hope. Lancelot had passed his final test – and after hardly any training too. Arthur might have been fed up for a moment at his defeat, but he had soon acknowledged Lancelot's striking performance.

Merlin strained to listen as Uther drew Lancelot aside. 'You do us a great honour, Sir Lancelot,' the king was saying. 'The knighthood is the very foundation of Camelot.'

'The honour is all mine, sire,' Lancelot replied.

'Your father would be very proud.'

Merlin winced. He'd almost forgotten the dishonest foundation this victory was built upon. Lancelot looked very uncomfortable as he replied, 'Yes, sire.'

There was worse to come. 'I've not seen Lord Eldred for many years,' Uther continued. 'Longer than I'd imagined, it seems. Last time I saw him, he only had four sons.'

For a moment Merlin thought the new knight had frozen in fear. But he managed a weak smile. 'Well – here I am . . .'

Uther smiled. 'Indeed you are,' he said. 'And I've kept you too long already.' He

laid a reassuring hand on Lancelot's arm. 'Enjoy the celebrations.' And he left him to it.

Merlin relaxed. The danger was over. He watched happily as the knights swept up their latest member, bearing him towards the feast that had been laid on in his honour. Lancelot was smiling in joy and disbelief.

The warlock turned to Gaius. Surely even he could see how great this was. Surely he could finally appreciate that Merlin had done the right thing. 'Look at him, Gaius,' he said. 'Does Lancelot not deserve this moment?'

'I never said he didn't,' Gaius replied. 'But destiny and deserts are not the same thing. You played God, Merlin. You set him on a path of your choosing. Tonight you have brought him triumph, but who knows what the future may hold?'

Merlin turned towards Gaius and said with a smile, 'Yeah, I don't know what it said on your invitation, but on mine it said "celebration"!'

Gaius laughed. 'Point taken.'

After Gaius left, Merlin went over to Gwen. He couldn't help noticing that every time he looked at Lancelot, Lancelot seemed to be casting shy glances towards the maidservant — even though he was supposed to be talking to Prince Arthur.

'I think our Sir Lancelot may have eyes for you, Gwen,' Merlin commented with a grin.

She looked embarrassed. 'Don't be silly.'

He laughed. 'So what if he does? Would that really be so bad?'

'He's not really my type,' Gwen said.

'Well, there's a surprise. Sometimes, Guinevere,' Merlin said in his best elder-brother voice, 'I wonder if you'd know what your type was if he was standing right next to you.' He'd seen Lancelot and Gwen together and was sure they were perfect for each other. And he knew Gwen wasn't interested in any other man – why, she seemed to spend most of her spare time with Merlin; there wasn't time for her to meet anyone else!

But Gwen wasn't going to discuss it. She shushed him as Arthur banged on a table for silence. The prince stood up and announced, 'Ladies and gentlemen, please join me in a toast. To our new recruit – our new Knight of Camelot. Sir Lancelot.' He raised his tankard and everyone cheered.

Merlin grinned. This was meant to be. And he'd made it happen.

But Merlin wouldn't have felt so pleased with himself if he'd realized just how suspicious the king had been about Eldred's mysterious 'fifth son'.

Uther had sent Lancelot's seal of nobility to the court genealogist, Geoffrey of Monmouth – the very records keeper under whose nose the seal had been crafted. At that moment Geoffrey was working away by candlelight, poring over the book Merlin had used earlier, preparing to deliver his expert opinion to the king.

The extent of the celebrations was obvious the next morning when Merlin and Lancelot staggered down to breakfast. Gaius was ready for them with a remedy for all the ale. 'Don't look at it, don't smell it, just down it in one,' he said, handing them each a beaker.

They grimaced and obeyed.

'Better?' Gaius asked. They shuddered, but nodded. 'Good. Can't have you nodding off first day on the job, Lancelot.'

'That's *Sir* Lancelot if you don't mind,' put in Merlin.

They were all laughing when the guards burst through the door and grabbed Lancelot.

'Stop! What are you doing?' yelled Merlin as the knight was dragged out of the room, but the guards made no reply.

★

For the second time in only a few hours, Lancelot found himself on his knees in front of the king. But this time Uther was not smiling, and neither was Prince Arthur, who stood beside him. The court genealogist on the king's other side held the Northumbrian seal in his hand.

'These credentials are faked,' the king hissed at the humiliated knight. 'The forgery is excellent – but there is no record of a fifth son of Lord Eldred of Northumbria. Therefore you lied. Do you deny it?'

Lancelot hung his head. 'No, sire.' How could he deny the truth? The truth was something he should never have turned his back on in the first place. But he had opened his heart to that one small lie – and it had led here.

Uther's voice rose, harsh and unforgiving.

'You have broken the First Code of Camelot. You have brought shame upon yourself and upon us. You are not worthy of the knighthood bestowed upon you. You never were. And you never will be.' He turned to the guards. 'Get him out of my sight.'

Lancelot could not meet Arthur's eye as he was dragged from the room. The shame and humiliation were almost unbearable, but worst of all was the knowledge that he had betrayed this man whom he admired so much.

Arthur watched with concern as Lancelot was led away. He felt torn. Lancelot had lied to him, made a fool out of him – yet that nobility he had sensed in the man; that bravery, that comradeship: they were not things he could be mistaken about. 'Sire . . .' he said.

The king, pouring himself a drink, did

not look at his son as he replied. 'Do you contest my judgement?'

Arthur knew he had to tread carefully. 'His deception was inexcusable. But he meant no harm, sire, I am sure of it. He only wished to serve.'

'The First Code is a sacred bond of trust. It is what binds the knights together.' Now the king turned and looked his son straight in the eye. 'How can you trust a man who's lied to you?'

And Arthur had no answer to that. A man of honour wouldn't lie. He was certain that Lancelot was a man of honour. Yet Lancelot had lied. The problem was insoluble.

Arthur might have understood more had he heard a conversation that took place between Merlin and the imprisoned Lancelot shortly afterwards.

The guilt was eating Merlin up inside and he could hardly bear to look at the disgraced warrior. 'I don't know what to say to you . . .' the boy began.

'Say nothing, my friend,' said Lancelot kindly. 'You're not to blame.'

'Oh yes I am! I pushed you. I made you lie.'

The other shook his head. What made it worse for Merlin was that even now, Lancelot was displaying the dignity and gallantry that marked out the best of knights! 'The choice was mine,' the man said. 'My punishment is mine to bear, and mine to bear alone.'

Merlin looked at him sadly. 'I wish there was something I could do.'

'There is,' Lancelot replied. 'You can stop blaming yourself.'

But Merlin knew that Lancelot was asking for the impossible.

CHAPTER SEVEN

THE GRIFFIN COMES TO CAMELOT

When Merlin returned to the doctor's chambers he was convinced that Gaius' first words would be 'I told you so'. But Gaius had other things to tell him. He had made a discovery.

'I've been scouring my books trying to find the beast that you and the villagers described. None matched it. But then I realized my mistake. Here – come and take a look at this.' Merlin hurried over to see the page that Gaius had indicated. 'I was looking for the creature in the wrong place – in the records of all known living things in the kingdom. But then I thought, what about creatures only recorded in legend, in myth? And I discovered this.' He pointed to an illustration: an animal with the head and wings of an eagle and the body of a lion.

'That's it!' Merlin cried. 'That's the monster!'

Suddenly the warning bell began to toll. Horrified, Merlin and Gaius ran to the window – just in time to see the people in the city below running for cover and screaming in terror. Now Gaius was able to confirm his identification at first hand. Because the monster had come to Camelot.

Arthur ran out, a shield in one hand and a spear in the other. Behind him came a

group of knights, their weapons raised. The
prince took up position in the middle of
the square. 'On me!' he yelled, and the
others hurried into formation alongside
him.

The monster saw them and swooped.
'Defence!' shouted Arthur, and each
knight crouched down, shield held above
him. The creature flew across them, its
talons scraping along the sea of shields.
The gale from the beat of its wings
knocked them to the ground. The beast
circled, and as the knights scrambled to
their feet it landed in front of them.

'Charge!' Arthur yelled. The knights
followed his lead, weapons at the ready.
The prince ran in close as the monster
reared on its hind legs, screeching in fury.
He lunged with his spear, a killing blow . . .

. . . and stared in horror as the spear
shattered on the creature's belly.

The monster pounced on the weaponless prince, knocking him off his feet. A quick-thinking guard threw Arthur a burning torch and he grabbed it desperately, swinging it at the creature – which shied from the flames and finally retreated, soaring away over the palace.

Breathlessly, Arthur watched it go. He was relieved to have chased it away from his people, but this was no victory. The monster lived to kill another day.

The king did not share in his son's gloom. 'You proved today that your knights are the best in the land,' he said proudly as he led Arthur into the council chamber, where Gaius and Merlin stood waiting.

'All I know is that it's still out there,' the prince replied.

'Then let's not wait for it,' said Uther. 'The kingdom has been menaced by this creature for too long. We finish this now.'

Gaius stepped forward. 'Sire, if I may . . .'

The king turned to him. 'Yes, Gaius?'

'I've been researching this creature, sire,' the doctor told him. 'I believe it to be a Griffin – a creature of magic.'

Uther's face became hard and angry. 'I don't have time for this, physician,' he snarled.

But Gaius had faced the king's wrath many times and wasn't cowed. 'It is born of magic, sire. And it can only be killed by magic.'

'You are mistaken,' growled Uther. 'It is a creature of flesh and blood like any other. Arthur proved that today.'

The prince stepped forward. 'I'm not so sure, Father. I think there might be some truth in what he says. Our weapons seemed useless against it.'

But magic had been mentioned, and that meant the king would shut his ears to all argument. 'Useless? I think not. No, it has tasted our steel once. The next time will be its last. You will ride out with your knights and finish this tonight!'

★

Merlin and Gaius returned to the doctor's rooms. But as they left the council chamber, Merlin had seen Arthur's expression. The prince would not speak out against his father any more, and he would never refuse to face the creature − if there was the slightest chance of destroying the killer, Arthur had to take it. But Merlin could see that Gaius' words had worried him.

Their only hope was that Gaius was wrong − but that didn't happen very often. 'Is it true?' he said desperately. 'That the Griffin can only be killed by magic?'

The doctor nodded. 'Yes, Merlin. I am certain of it. If Arthur rides out against it . . . he will die.'

'Then Uther must be made to see reason,' Merlin said. But he knew as he said it that such a thing was impossible.

'Where magic is concerned, our king is blind to reason.' Gaius looked Merlin straight in the eye. 'And yet magic is our only hope.'

It took Merlin a moment to realize what Gaius was suggesting. The physician always tried to stop him practising magic; now suddenly he was encouraging him to use it! Merlin's first reaction was a surge of joy at the chance to do what he loved, what he did best. But almost instantly other thoughts crowded it out. He'd seen the monster. It was enormous, deadly, indestructible. He didn't have magic that powerful. To go against it would mean almost certain death – and this time there would be no Lancelot to save him. 'There has to be another way,' he said.

Gaius was firm. 'This is the only way.'

How could he be so calm when he was telling Merlin to go to his death! 'Do you even care what happens to me?' the boy cried. '"Oh, just do this, Merlin, do that, Merlin! Go and kill the Griffin,

Merlin, while I sit and warm my feet by the fire!"' He knew the words were unfair, but he was sick of being the one who took all the risks. Oh, the things he had faced! And it wasn't simply that he'd fought so many sorcerers and monsters; if anyone discovered what he'd done he would be executed!

Gaius looked shocked, then hurt, and guilt swept through Merlin as the old man addressed him. 'Merlin, you are the only thing I care about in all this world. I would give my life for you without a thought. But for what? *I* cannot save Arthur. It is not *my* destiny.'

'Sorry,' Merlin whispered, taken aback by the sincerity

MERLIN, YOU ARE THE ONLY THING I CARE ABOUT IN ALL THIS WORLD.

SORRY.

of the doctor's words. Gaius was right. Destiny had called on Merlin for these tasks. It was the price he paid for his powers. Whatever the risks were, he had to act. He had to save Arthur. He turned to Gaius, newly determined. 'We have to find a way to kill that thing. And we don't have much time.'

CHAPTER EIGHT
TO MEET DEATH

The knights were busying themselves, preparing to fight the Griffin. Swords were being sharpened, horses were being made ready. Their leader should have been with them, but Arthur had something else on his mind. There was something he could not leave undone, if he was riding to his doom.

He opened the door of Lancelot's cell. Lancelot leaped to his feet, and Arthur felt anger swelling inside him as he looked at the man who had deceived him – the man who should have been fighting by his side. 'I should have known!' he shouted. 'How could I have been so stupid? You don't sound like a knight, you don't even look like a knight . . .'

Lancelot bowed his head in shame. 'I'm sorry.'

'I'm sorry too,' the prince told him. 'Because, Lancelot, you fight like a knight. And I need . . . *Camelot* needs . . .' He trailed off. What more could he say? What use were recriminations now?

'The creature,' Lancelot said. 'I heard it outside . . .'

'We could not kill it,' said Arthur. 'I have never faced its like.'

'I faced it myself, sire,' Lancelot told him, 'some days past. I struck it full square. I wondered how it endured.'

Arthur looked at him gravely. 'There are

those that believe this creature, this Griffin, is a creature of magic. That only magic can destroy it.'

'Do you believe this?' asked Lancelot.

Despite the man's deference, despite everything Arthur knew about him, the prince could not rid himself of the impression that he was talking to an equal. He found himself answering Lancelot candidly. 'It doesn't matter what I believe. The use of magic is not permitted. The knights must prevail with steel and sinew alone.' *But these would not be enough* . . .

'Sire—' Lancelot began, but the prince cut him off.

'There's a horse waiting outside.' Lancelot's face lit up, but Arthur had to disillusion him. 'Take it and never return to this place.'

'No!' Lancelot was distraught. 'Please, it's not my freedom I seek. I only wish to serve with honour. Let me ride with you, sire!'

'I cannot!' Arthur would have given a lot to grant the man's wish, but he knew that a worse fate than imprisonment would greet Lancelot if he did so. The king did not like to be defied. Arthur himself was taking a great risk doing this much. 'My father knows nothing of this,' he told Lancelot. 'I release you myself, but I can do no more. Now go, before I change my mind.'

Arthur was relieved when Lancelot left the cell. Deep inside, though, he felt a twinge of disappointment in the man. He hadn't expected him to give in so easily.

But Arthur hadn't been looking at the man as he walked out. He hadn't seen the determination on his face. Lancelot hadn't given in at all . . .

★

Gwen was sitting sewing by candlelight when a knock came at the door. To her astonishment, she looked up to see Lancelot entering the room. 'I'm sorry to disturb you, my lady,' he said. 'But I need weapons, armour – the best you've got.'

She rose to her feet. 'But what's this all about?'

'Arthur stands in mortal peril. I must do what I can to protect him. It's my duty,' he told her, 'knight or not.'

And as Gwen met his eyes, she saw such belief in them, such certainty, such goodness. Feelings welled up inside her – feelings she had never experienced before. She caught her breath, astonished by their intensity.

'Guinevere, if I should not return—' Lancelot began.

She cut across him. 'Don't go, Lancelot, please.' Suddenly the idea of letting him leave seemed more painful than she could bear. And yet she knew that he would go; would face death a thousand times over if his duty demanded it. The man she saw in front of her could do nothing else.

Despair threatened to overwhelm Merlin. Together with Gaius, he had located the spell he needed – a spell to enchant a weapon. Only with such a weapon could the Griffin be killed.

But the stronger the creature, the stronger the magic needed to destroy it – and the Griffin was a very strong creature indeed. Merlin had never even tried to cast such a powerful spell before.

'You have it within you, I know you do,' Gaius told him. He handed Merlin an ordinary knife. 'Here. Try.'

So Merlin tried. '*Bregdan anweald gafeluec . . .*' he intoned with care, directing the force of his mind at the simple blade.

Nothing happened.

He tried again. Still nothing. Despair rose up inside him. What if he just wasn't good enough? What if his powers were too weak? This was a spell for the greatest of sorcerers, those who'd honed their skills over decades, not some boy who fancied himself a warlock.

He tried again, focusing all that he had on the knife, but in vain.

Gaius gave him an unconvincing smile of reassurance. 'There's plenty of time,' he said, but Merlin knew that was just not true. Arthur was riding out even now. And if Arthur died because Merlin was not good enough—

Suddenly the door burst open. Gwen ran into the room. 'Merlin! Lancelot's riding out to kill the Griffin!'

'He's *what*?!' Merlin yelled.

Time had just run out.

★

Lancelot knew he was probably riding out to his death. But what else could he do? He might not be a knight, but that did not mean he could not behave as a knight should behave. Arthur needed him and the kingdom needed him, and there was nothing more to be said.

As he saddled his horse, he spotted Merlin running towards him. He expected the boy to try to persuade him not to go, so Merlin's actual words came as a surprise: 'I'm coming with you,' he announced.

'No, you're not,' Lancelot said simply. He admired the youth's bravery – but Merlin was not a soldier. He should not throw his life away.

But Merlin insisted. 'Arthur needs all the help he can get.'

Lancelot looked into the boy's eyes and realized there was no point in arguing. He

was not the only one who believed in duty
– he could see that Merlin felt he had to do
this. He could not stand in the boy's way.

Together, Merlin and Lancelot rode out of
Camelot, following the tracks of Arthur
and his knights. Merlin went over the
words of the spell in his mind. He still
couldn't make it work, but he had nothing
else to try.

Mist shrouded the trees as they entered
the forest, plunging them into a nightmare
world of grey. Suddenly there came a great
screech, then shouts – and screams. The
knights had found the Griffin. Or was it
the Griffin that had found them . . . ?

Merlin and Lancelot spurred their horses
forward, weaving their way through the
trees. There was a flash of red in the mist
– the broken body of a knight. Merlin
leaped down from his horse and ran towards

it, Lancelot following. Here was another knight, and another, but Merlin had no time to mourn for them as he sought for the face he dreaded finding . . .

The mist parted, and there it was. Merlin stopped breathing. Slumped against a tree was Arthur Pendragon.

Merlin had failed.

CHAPTER NINE
VICTORY AND LOSS

Merlin threw himself down by the prince, frantically checking for signs of life. Yes! He allowed himself to breathe again. Arthur was still alive!

There was no time for celebration, though. The Griffin was still out there.

A screech, a flap of wings ... Lancelot was already back on his horse, lance lowered, riding towards the beast.

It was now or never. Summoning every scrap of magic inside him, Merlin began to intone the spell: '*Bregdan anweald gafeluec . . .*'

Nothing happened.

Nearer and nearer rode Lancelot. The Griffin swooped. Merlin tried again. If he did not succeed this time, the monster would be claiming another victim. Not only would Camelot lose a great warrior; Merlin would lose a friend. Lancelot was a good man, a great man, as noble as Arthur himself, and Merlin felt honoured to be by his side in battle. *He would not let Lancelot die . . .*

Could he be drawing power from the air, the trees, the very earth beneath his feet . . . ? Because suddenly there was so much within him, he couldn't contain it. '*Bregdan anweald gafeluec!*' The heat surged through his body and his eyes turned golden as he channelled it out towards the weapon in Lancelot's hand.

The force hit the lance, blue-white energy engulfing it like flames. Merlin laughed with joy as he saw his success; as he saw the weapon hit the beast; as the creature fell ...

The energy faded; the lance was just a lance again.

Lancelot's eyes were wide with amazement as he turned to look at Merlin. But Merlin had no time to talk. He could hear footsteps in the distance – Arthur had come round. The prince must believe this was Lancelot's work alone.

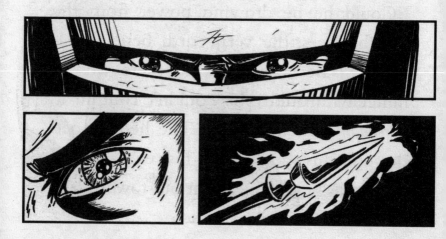

As he rode off towards the castle, eager not to be spotted, he heard Arthur's amazed shout. 'You did it, Lancelot! You killed it!'

All would be well. The Griffin was no longer a threat, and Lancelot would be a hero.

Merlin had a moment of feeling like a hero too as he stumbled, exhausted, into Gaius' chambers and saw the look of joy on the old doctor's face. He also suddenly realized how much it had cost Gaius to send him on that path.

But thank goodness he had. Arthur was saved — and Lancelot would

be revered throughout Camelot, just as he deserved.

But later, as Merlin and Lancelot waited outside the council chambers for Lancelot's fate to be decided, it seemed that there would be no praise for the warrior, nor even any thanks.

'His actions change nothing!' Uther was shouting. The triumph on his face had turned to rage as he learned that it was not Arthur who had defeated the monster but the man whom he had imprisoned. The man who had lied. 'He broke the Code,' the king reminded his son.

But Arthur would not listen to any more insults against Lancelot. 'He laid down his life for me! He served with honour!' he cried.

'I see you feel strongly about this, Arthur.' The king looked almost taken aback.

'Under the circumstances . . . a pardon, perhaps.'

But Arthur wanted more. 'Not good enough, Father. You must restore Lancelot to his rightful place – as a Knight of Camelot.'

That was too much for Uther. 'Never! The law is the law! The Code bends for no man.'

And Arthur realized, not for the first time, how different he and his father were. For Arthur, a law that could never change was not a just law at all. 'Then the Code is wrong,' he shouted.

'They'll restore your knighthood, of course they will,' said Merlin with a confidence he didn't feel. 'You killed the Griffin.'

'But I didn't kill the Griffin.' Lancelot stopped pacing the corridor and turned to his friend. '*You* did.'

Merlin laughed nervously. 'That's ridiculous.'

'*Bregdan anweald?* I heard you. I saw you,' Lancelot said.

Merlin was horrified. It wasn't that he didn't trust the man. But . . . well, the knights were pledged to fight sorcery wherever it might be found, and Lancelot believed so strongly in the knight's code of honour. Would he feel honour-bound to tell Uther of Merlin's true nature?

Merlin's fears lasted only a second. Lancelot smiled at him. 'Don't worry. Your secret's safe with me.' He drew himself up. 'But I cannot take the credit for what I did not do.' He walked to the door of the council chamber. 'There'll be no more lies. No more deceit.'

The door crashed open. No sooner had Lancelot stepped through than two guards grabbed his arms, ready to drag him out of the king's sight.

Arthur and Uther turned in surprise as the man fought against his captors. 'Let me speak!'

To Arthur's astonishment the king raised a hand to stay the guards. 'Wait. I'll hear him.'

Lancelot bowed his head in thanks. 'Forgive me, sire. But I come to bid you farewell,' he said. 'I lied to you both, and now there is conflict between you. I cannot bear that burden. As you should not bear mine.' He lifted his eyes to the prince. 'I must start again, far from here. Then maybe one day fate shall grant me another chance to prove myself a worthy knight of Camelot.'

Arthur felt a pang of regret, sharper than any he'd known. Every word this man said showed his worthiness. 'But, Lancelot, you have already proved that to us,' he said.

The other shook his head. 'But I must prove it to myself.'

As Lancelot left the room, Arthur found it hard to shake the feeling that he'd just lost the best friend he never had.

The prince was not the only one to feel Lancelot's departure keenly. Elsewhere in the palace, Gwen watched from a window as he rode away. Her heart told her that she had lost something very precious.

But Gwen was a servant, and she had a job to do. She turned from the window and began to tidy Morgana's room.

'Perhaps you were right. Perhaps I should never have got involved,' Merlin said to Gaius as they too watched Lancelot ride into the distance.

But Gaius shook his head. 'No, Merlin.

I was wrong. Lancelot needed you. And you needed Lancelot. Your destinies were entwined.'

'Will he ever return?' Merlin asked, knowing an answer was impossible.

Gaius shrugged. 'That I cannot say . . .'

They watched until the galloping figure disappeared into the trees. 'Till the next time, then,' whispered Merlin. 'Sir Lancelot . . .'

CHAPTER TEN

A MYSTERIOUS STRANGER

Over the weeks that followed, Gwen tried hard to put Lancelot from her mind. One evening a vast bunch of lilies was delivered to the castle, and she felt disappointed when she saw that they were for Morgana, not her. Of course, why would they be for her? Lancelot had probably not given her another thought. And yet she had seen what was in his eyes as he bade her farewell, and knew that they had connected for ever . . .

No more regrets. She picked up the flowers with a smile on her face, and hurried off to Morgana's room.

'Who are they from?' Morgana asked as Gwen arranged them in a vase by the bed.

'I don't know,' said Gwen. 'Who would you like them to be from?'

Morgana laughed. 'A tall dark stranger,' she said.

Gwen wished her mistress a good night and turned to snuff out the candles.

In the resulting darkness, neither maid nor mistress saw a black beetle crawl out from the heart of a flower. It dropped onto

Morgana's pillow, and scurried towards her ear ...

Outside, a stranger was watching and waiting. He was tall, although he was not dark. If it were not for the terrible scars that ravaged his face, he would have been handsome. The lilies were his gift.

The gift of death ...

Gaius was close to despair. For two days Morgana had lain in a trance. It was as though she were asleep, but nothing the physician tried could rouse her from her deep slumber.

'Her body seems to have closed down,' he told the king.

'But why?' Uther demanded. 'You don't

have an answer, do you?'

Gaius didn't. 'I fear she may have some form of inflammation of the brain, possibly caused by an infection,' he said. Based on all his scientific knowledge, that was the only theory he had. But he had to admit to himself that it was really little more than a guess. 'Rest assured, I will do everything in my power to cure her, sire.'

The physician doubted that even his best would be enough to save the girl. But he did not dare admit that to the king.

Merlin had been waiting outside Morgana's room and hurried over as Gaius came out. Gaius turned his face away, but he knew that the boy had already read his expression. 'She is all but dead, Merlin,' he admitted sadly.

'No!' the boy cried. 'You're going to cure her – you *have* to!'

Gaius appreciated his faith, but knew it

was misplaced. Only a miracle would save her now, and he did not keep miracles in his medicine chest.

Merlin leaned forward. 'I was wondering . . .'

'What?' asked Gaius, although he had a very good idea what Merlin's idea would be.

'Well, maybe I could . . . help.'

'If you're suggesting magic,' the doctor said with stern disapproval, 'this is not a magical illness. It must be cured by conventional means.' He sighed. 'We just have to keep trying.'

Prince Arthur left the palace that evening, a frown on his face. A stranger had been asking for him, but he was in no mood to deal with trivialities. He was already on a short fuse; Merlin had been annoying him enormously by pacing up and down all afternoon. He was worried enough himself without having to deal with other people's anxieties.

'What's your business here?' the prince barked as he approached the hooded man.

The figure turned, and Arthur had to repress a shudder as he saw the terrible scars on the man's face. It looked as though his flesh had been melted like wax. But he had little sympathy to waste on a stranger – all he could think of was Morgana. They fought, they bickered, she drove him up the wall . . . but the idea of a world without her was too terrible to contemplate.

To his astonishment, the man had the gall to speak of her. 'My name is Edwin Muirden, and I have a remedy to cure all ills,' he said. 'I hear the Lady Morgana is gravely ill.'

'That is no concern of yours,' snapped Arthur.

The man seemed to take no offence at the prince's bluntness. 'I may be able to help her,' he said.

Arthur had no time for quacks or charlatans. 'Our physician has the matter in hand,' he said, walking away.

'I'll be at the inn,' the stranger called after him. 'In case you change your mind . . .'

The morning sun rose on three people who had not slept, and one whose sleep seemed eternal.

Gaius left Morgana's bedside and turned to the king and Arthur. He dreaded the news he must impart, but he no longer had a choice. Those who loved her must be prepared for the worst.

'I cannot preserve her life for much longer,' he said. 'She has hours, maybe less.'

'We cannot let her die!' Arthur cried in anguish.

'Arthur, please,' said Uther. Gaius had never known the king look so defeated, so frail.

But the prince would not be quieted. 'There's a man – he came to the castle yesterday. He claims he can cure her.'

'That's ridiculous. He doesn't know what's wrong with her,' Uther said.

'He says he has a remedy to cure all ills.'

Gaius felt a huge sympathy for the young prince. Desperation was making him clutch at any possibility. But the physician had studied medicine for many, many years. He knew that there was no such thing as 'a remedy to cure all ills'.

'Impossible,' he said.

Arthur wouldn't listen. 'But for Morgana's sake, surely we should at least hear him out. I mean, what do we have to lose? Please, Father!'

The doctor didn't want Uther to have any false hopes. 'Probably some charlatan hoping for a quick shilling.'

'I don't care!' Arthur shouted. 'If she's about to die, then what harm can it do? Give him his shilling! If there's one chance in a million he can save her, then why not?'

Uther turned to Gaius, and that touched the physician's heart more than anything. For the king to be unsure, even for a moment . . . Gaius shrugged his shoulders, giving in. It could do no good. But then, it could do no harm. Morgana was past saving. And he did not want Uther to be for ever haunted by the thought that he had left something undone, something that might have worked.

'Send for him,' Uther ordered.

Arthur left the room to fetch the mysterious stranger.

SEND FOR HIM.

CHAPTER ELEVEN

A REMEDY TO CURE ALL ILLS

Merlin was frustrated. There was nothing he could do – and he seemed to be getting on everyone's nerves. However many times he asked, Gaius refused to let him use magic. Arthur couldn't bear anyone's company. And he wasn't even allowed to see Morgana.

But he'd taken to hanging around outside her room, in the hope of finding a way to help – or at least of discovering what was happening. He was there when Arthur hurried off down the corridor, and he was there when Uther and Gaius came out shortly afterwards. For a moment he feared the worst, but he heard Gaius say something about 'remedy' and became quite excited. Had they found a cure, then? He followed quietly behind until they reached the council chamber, then waited a moment before slipping into the room after them.

A man was standing at the end of the chamber. He sank to one knee as the king approached. 'Edwin Muirden, sire. Physician and loyal servant.'

Gaius was looking at the man with obvious curiosity. 'Have we met before?'

I DOUBT YOU WOULD FORGET A FACE LIKE MINE, SIR.

Edwin smiled as he rose. 'I doubt you would forget a face like mine, sir.' Seeing the man's scarred face, Merlin had to acknowledge that was true.

'Do you really believe you have a remedy?' Uther demanded.

'There are not many ills that I have not seen and successfully treated, sire,' Edwin said. 'So when I heard of the Lady Morgana's sickness I felt honour-bound to offer my services.'

Merlin felt a rush of excitement. Could this be the miracle they'd all longed for?

But Gaius did not seem so enthusiastic. 'You say you have an antidote for *everything*?' he asked, clearly sceptical.

'Yes. Although it is not quite as simple as that . . .'

'Gaius is the court physician,' Uther told Edwin.

Edwin turned to the old doctor. 'You are indeed a legend, sir,' he said. 'I am delighted to meet you. I am indeed curious to know what it is that has affected the lady.'

'An infection of the brain,' Gaius answered. 'I have treated her with yarrow, and with rosemary to stimulate cerebral circulation.'

'Interesting,' said Edwin.

Arthur jumped on that. 'Why, what would you suggest?'

The man waved away any suggestion of criticism. 'No, no, no, that is all fine. All good.' He paused. 'If that *is* the right diagnosis.'

Merlin's attitude towards Edwin underwent a sudden change. How dare he walk into

Camelot and start questioning Gaius' abilities? Gaius was the greatest doctor he knew. True, he was the only doctor he knew ... But since coming to Camelot, Merlin had watched Gaius treat so many people, and his skill and knowledge were unquestionable.

'What would your diagnosis be?' Uther asked Edwin.

'Well, without examining the patient ...'

It was rapidly agreed that Edwin should be allowed to see Morgana. 'And consider my manservant at your disposal,' added Arthur, spotting Merlin lurking by the door.

Edwin bowed deeply. 'I will start work immediately,' he said.

Merlin helped Edwin to set up his equipment in a guest room. The instruments were like nothing he'd ever seen before, even in Gaius' chambers — strange metal devices the purposes of which he couldn't guess. Edwin told him they were originally designed for alchemy, the process by which men attempted to turn base metals into gold.

One thing seemed out of place, though: a carved wooden box with a runic inscription on the lid. Merlin picked it up curiously, but Edwin snatched it out of his hands. 'Yes, we'll need that,' he said. 'Now, we must hurry to the Lady Morgana. Before it's too late.'

Uther, Arthur and Gaius were already with Morgana when they arrived, but Edwin asked everyone to leave. To Merlin's disappointment, that included him — he'd been looking forward to seeing what these peculiar instruments were for. Gaius too expressed an interest in staying, but Edwin would have none of it. 'I require peace and privacy,' he explained.

Gaius reluctantly left the room. With a last look at Edwin – and the sleeping Morgana – Merlin followed.

Gwen was trying to keep busy. She had lost Lancelot, and now it seemed she would lose the mistress she adored. If she stopped for even a second, terrible thoughts crowded into her head and made her want to weep.

She faithfully stayed close to her beloved Morgana, tidying and retidying her room even though it didn't need it, cleaning already clean things again and again. When the king was present she retreated to an anteroom, but spent every possible minute near her mistress' side.

Now she opened the door of the anteroom and entered Morgana's chamber again. To her surprise, she saw a purple-robed man leaning over Morgana, seemingly examining her ear.

He stood quickly, rounding on her. 'Why are you spying on me?'

'I wasn't,' Gwen stammered. 'I'm Morgana's maidservant.'

The man looked at her for a moment. 'Then bring me some water,' he said finally. Gwen hesitated. 'Now! Unless you want to be responsible for her death!'

Scared, Gwen hurried from the room.

She would have been even more scared had she stayed. What Edwin did next was not the act of a physician.

He laid the carved wooden box on Morgana's pillow and gripped a pair of

tweezers. Slowly he began to chant the words of a spell. As he did so, a black beetle scurried out of the girl's ear, bringing with it a trickle of blood. The insect was soon seized by Edwin's tweezers. With a satisfied smile, he placed it in the wooden box that teemed with its fellows. Then he wiped the blood from Morgana's ear with a piece of gauze, and hurried off to tell Uther that all was well.

The king's ward had been cured.

CHAPTER TWELVE

GOOD NEWS, BAD NEWS

'Great news, your majesty!' Uther, Arthur, Gaius and Merlin all looked up at Edwin's call. He was hurrying towards them with a smile on his face. 'You will be glad to hear it's not an inflammation of the brain,' he continued. 'It is a cerebral haemorrhage — there is bleeding inside her brain.'

'I don't think so—' Gaius began, but Edwin cut across him.

'I found this trace of blood in her ear.' He showed them the red-spotted piece of gauze. 'The severity depends on the site and volume of the bleed. If not treated it can lead to coma – and, eventually, death.'

The king turned on Gaius. 'How did you miss this?'

HOW DID YOU MISS THIS?

'I didn't see any blood,' the physician said.

Edwin gave him a patient but pitying look. 'Please. Just thank the fates that you didn't administer more rosemary to stimulate the circulation. Can you imagine what that might have done?'

Uther looked enquiringly at Gaius, and

the doctor was forced to explain. 'It may have increased the bleed.'

The king turned his back on his trusty servant, looking only to Edwin now. 'Is there a cure?'

Edwin beamed. 'See for yourself . . .'

They followed him up the stairs to Morgana's room. And there she was, sitting up in bed, looking weak but well.

Uther ran to her side, grasping her hand, kissing her forehead, unable to control his joy. His ward had been returned to him.

Nothing would be too good for the man who had saved her.

Gaius left Morgana's room, but did not return to his own chambers. Instead he waited patiently for Edwin to leave too, then hurried after him. The man did not seem overly pleased to see Gaius, although he politely accepted his congratulations.

'She was all but dead and you brought her back to life,' Gaius said. 'How exactly did you do that?'

Edwin smiled modestly. 'I have developed an elixir for the treatment of just such an ailment,' he said.

'I'd love to know the ingredients,' Gaius told him.

The other spread his hands in regret. 'It is not yet perfected. You must give me more time before I make it public.'

He turned away, but Gaius was not ready to let him go. 'The injury to your face . . .'

'It happened when I was very young,' Edwin said.

'Perhaps it was I that treated you for it.'

Edwin shook his head firmly. 'I told you before – we've never met.'

'Yes, of course,' Gaius said. But after Edwin had walked on, the doctor still did not return to his chambers. He headed instead towards the Hall of Records, where his old friend, Geoffrey of Monmouth, held sway.

He wanted to view the court records from the time of the Great Purge – but to his immense frustration, Geoffrey refused to let him see the sealed documents. 'Uther has forbidden it,' he insisted, despite the physician's pleas.

Gaius had no choice but to give in. But he was certain he would find the answers he sought in the history of that time. The time when Uther had killed every magic-user in the land.

He feared that the past might have come back to haunt them.

'Name your reward,' said Uther. With his ward seated beside him, the king was ready to be generous.

But in front of him, Edwin Muirden shook his head modestly. 'I desire nothing more than the good health of my patient, sire. I will wait until the Lady Morgana is fully recovered and then I will be on my way.'

Uther rose to his feet. 'Why don't you stay a while?' he suggested. 'You could live here, at the palace.'

Edwin looked tempted, but again shook his head. 'No. I . . . I feel I would be trespassing. And you already have a court physician.'

The king waved aside his objections. 'I'm sure Gaius would be glad of your help.' As Edwin began to demur again, he carried on, 'Think about it. Dine with me later and give me your decision.'

Edwin bowed deeply. 'To dine with your majesty would be reward in itself.'

★

Merlin had found a new hero. All his indignation on Gaius' behalf had vanished the moment Edwin had cured Morgana; the new arrival could now do no wrong in Merlin's eyes.

He was also very keen to learn more about Edwin's fascinating equipment. He hoped the man would show him what all the different items were for. So as soon as he'd completed his chores he hurried off to the guest chambers in the hope that he'd find Edwin there.

He knocked, but there was no reply. Of course, it was always possible that the man was too busy to hear him. It couldn't hurt to look inside . . .

Merlin pushed open the door. There was no sign of Edwin, but on the table his instruments glinted invitingly. The warlock felt drawn towards them. Hurrying over,

he began to examine the strange devices. And there, in the middle of them all, was the carved wooden box.

Merlin couldn't resist it. He picked it up and carefully opened the lid.

It was full of glittering black beetles. Dead ones, it seemed. Merlin was disappointed. Were they perhaps some ingredient for a potion? He couldn't think what else a load of insects could have to do with medicine.

But there were the runes on the box's lid. Perhaps they would tell him something.

 He closed the box and studied the inscription. 'Bedeode . . . re . . . arisan . . . ealdor . . .' he read aloud.

The box exploded

into sound: chitterings and scratchings. Merlin threw open the lid. The beetles had come to life.

'Very good,' said Edwin from the doorway.

Merlin spun round in horror. He had been caught doing magic, and there was nowhere to hide.

CHAPTER THIRTEEN
A MAGICAL MENTOR

Edwin came further into the room and took the box from Merlin's unresisting hands. '*Swefen*,' he intoned, and at that powerful word the chittering stopped. The beetles were once again still and lifeless.

Merlin was astounded. Edwin was a sorcerer, just like him! The only sorcerers he'd ever met before had been busy trying to kill people, often Merlin himself. Unless you counted Gaius, of course – Merlin had a strong suspicion that the physician had once practised magic, although he wouldn't admit it. But Merlin had never met anyone he could talk to as an equal, someone who would understand all about sorcery and not judge him. Could Edwin be that person?

But of course, it was too risky. In a land where magic could bring death, you couldn't afford to trust anyone. So when Edwin began to question him about what he'd seen, Merlin firmly denied that he'd been using magic at all.

Edwin didn't believe him, though. 'If you don't have magic, then how did you bring my beetles to life? Only magic can do such a thing.'

Merlin didn't know what to say. His denials weren't very convincing, but he didn't dare confess the truth.

Edwin held up the box, letting Merlin look inside again. 'I cured the Lady

Morgana with these little angels,' he said, indicating the insects. 'They repaired the damage to her brain. They saved her life.' He shut the box and walked away from the boy. 'Magic can be a force for good.'

'I know,' Merlin whispered.

Edwin turned on him. 'Then why do you fear it?'

'Uther has banned it,' Merlin said. 'It's not permitted.'

'Should I have let Morgana die?'

It was the sort of question that Merlin had considered a thousand times. When he had helped Lancelot with magic, things had gone horribly wrong – and yet in the end everything had turned out all right, and it was his magic that had saved Arthur and destroyed the deadly Griffin. Another time, he had saved someone's life, and a friend had been condemned to

death as a result — but again, his magic
had solved all the problems in the end. It
seemed to him that you could not worry
about what might happen, you just had
to solve the problem you saw in front of
you. If Edwin's magic had saved Morgana,
then how could it have been wrong to use
it? And this time, at least, there had been
no terrible consequences.

'No,' he said finally, in answer to the
question.

'People like us have a gift,' said Edwin.
'Do you not think
it should be used to
make this a better
world?'

PEOPLE LIKE US
HAVE A GIFT.

'Perhaps,' Merlin
said, realizing too late that he'd been tricked
into admitting his own magical nature. He
hurriedly looked away, leaning down to
clear up some powder he'd spilled earlier

when startled by Edwin's entrance.

'Don't waste your time picking that up!' Edwin said. And with a few magic words he sent the powder spinning into the air, a miniature tornado that swept back into the jar, leaving the table clear. 'Why waste a talent like that?' he said.

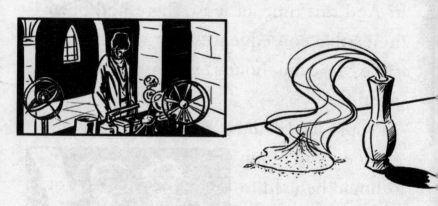

Merlin grinned. That spell would certainly come in useful when tidying Gaius' chambers. Not using magic *was* a waste, just like he'd always thought. If it wasn't for Gaius' nagging, his life would be so much easier – and more fun too. Because doing magic *was* fun.

He stared at the powder-filled vessel, and let the familiar heat rise inside him. The power built up behind his eyes, making them flash gold as he muttered a spell. The jar rose up, tipped to one side, and carefully emptied its powder into a bowl.

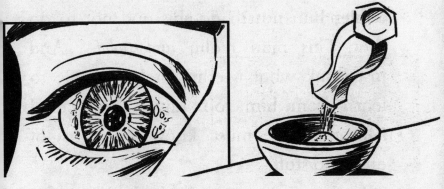

Edwin smiled, clearly impressed. 'What do you use this for?' he asked.

'Gaius doesn't like me to use it,' Merlin said hastily. His enthusiasm had made him go a bit too far.

Edwin looked pityingly at the boy. 'A gift like yours should be nurtured, practised, enjoyed. You need someone to help you, to encourage you. Imagine what we could achieve if we shared our knowledge . . .'

Merlin imagined. It was what he had always wanted. He was sick of having to hide his magic from everyone, sick of being thought useless and stupid, sick of Gaius telling him not to do this and not to do that. This man really *understood* . . . And just think what Merlin might be able to learn from him too. Edwin had cured Morgana: he must know all sorts of amazing stuff.

But it was too much to think about now. Things were moving too quickly. 'I should be getting back,' he told Edwin.

'Of course,' the sorcerer replied, seeming to understand Merlin's dilemma. 'But you must promise to keep our secret safe. People like you and me – we must look after each other.'

Merlin nodded. They left together, going

their separate ways at the door: Edwin to dine with the king, and Merlin to Gaius' chambers.

He was quite pleased to find the rooms empty when he arrived. Edwin's words had given him a lot to think about, and Gaius just wouldn't understand.

But the old physician might have understood more than Merlin supposed. Because at that moment he was searching through the court records from the time of the Great Purge. Geoffrey of Monmouth had relented and given his old and trusted friend access to the forbidden volumes. 'I know you wouldn't ask if it wasn't important,' he'd said. 'I cannot deny you this one request after the many kindnesses you have done me over the years.'

Gaius had assured him that a great deal was at stake. He was sure that the answers were all to be found in these books – and

he was right. The information they
contained shed a whole new light on
Edwin Muirden.

CHAPTER FOURTEEN
UNMASKED

The king was favourably impressed by Edwin's modesty and generosity. As they conversed, the man was keen to point out that Gaius' mistakes had only been natural, and that his own contribution was merely due to his good fortune in making the correct diagnosis. He was even quick to agree with the king that Gaius really was a great physician.

'And yet . . .' said Edwin. 'Well, that's what I don't understand . . .'

'What?' Uther asked.

The man hesitated. 'It's not for me to speak out of turn.'

But this man had saved Morgana's life. As Uther was quick to assure him, that meant he had earned the right to speak in any way he wished.

Reluctantly Edwin explained. 'Gaius has been prescribing sleeping draughts for Morgana – because of bad dreams, I understand. But those dreams should have been a warning. I believe they were a symptom of the illness, but the potions masked the problem, allowing it to develop to the point where . . .'

He trailed off, but Uther had no trouble completing the thought. 'The point where she nearly died.' The king thought for a moment. Gaius was an old and trusted servant – even a friend. But that was the point – he was old. He was making mistakes.

And the consequences of those mistakes could have been terrible. 'Will you undertake a review of his work?' he asked Edwin. 'Just to be on the safe side.'

The man looked embarrassed for a second, then nodded humbly. 'If it would put your mind at rest, sire,' he said.

Edwin was at work the next day when Gaius knocked on the door of his chambers. Without waiting for an answer, the physician entered.

'Your scar has healed well,' he said, staring with medical interest at the wax-like rivers on the younger man's face. 'I often  wondered what happened to that poor young boy.'

For the first time since his arrival in Camelot, Edwin seemed discomfited. 'I told you we'd never met before.'

But Gaius was quite certain. 'I didn't realize who you were until I checked the records,' he explained. 'You used your mother's maiden name. You're Gregor and Jaden's son.'

Edwin didn't try to deny it. 'They were friends of yours.'

'They were sorcerers.'

'They practised magic,' Edwin admitted. He stared pointedly at the doctor. 'And so did a lot of people back then, Gaius.'

'Uther will be furious when he finds out who you are,' the doctor replied.

'Fine.' To Gaius' surprise, Edwin swept across the room to the door. With a hand on the latch, he turned back to the physician. 'Shall we tell him? Yes, let's go and tell him. I know ... we could also tell him about Merlin.'

Gaius felt a rush of dread. 'Merlin?'

'You didn't know he was a sorcerer?' Edwin tutted and walked away from the door. 'I wonder what Uther will do. Probably have him burned.'

Still numb with shock, Gaius said, 'You would betray another sorcerer?'

Suddenly Edwin's anger exploded, his mask of self-control shattering. '*You* did! When you turned a blind eye and let my parents die at the hands of Uther. At least Merlin doesn't have a son who will try to rescue him from the flames!' He pointed a trembling finger at his scarred face – where the execution fires had melted his flesh.

'You're here to take revenge.' Gaius stated it as fact. 'You think I will sacrifice the king to save Merlin . . . ?'

'Think about it,' said Edwin. 'But if I find you've told one other person – including the boy – I will go straight to Uther.'

As Edwin stood before the king later that day, his emotions were once again hidden from view. No watcher would have dreamed that he was nurturing such a terrible hatred for the man in front of him. No watcher would have suspected that his reluctant criticisms of Gaius' work were anything but the genuine concerns of a fellow physician.

'With regret, I would have to say that my findings in the court medical records were not satisfactory, sire,' he told Uther. 'Gaius is a great man – thorough, dedicated – but his methods are outdated. He has failed to keep up with the latest developments, and this has led to a number of errors.'

'Gaius has served me well for twenty-five years,' the king pointed out.

'And one cannot blame him for the infirmity those years have brought.' Edwin was carefully confirming the suspicions that he'd placed in Uther's mind earlier – that Gaius was too old for the job.

The king nodded thoughtfully. 'Perhaps it's time to lighten his burdens. Have you given any more thought to my offer – of staying here, in the palace?'

'Oh yes,' said Edwin, not a trace of exultation showing on his face as yet more pieces of his plan fell into place. 'Yes, sire, I have . . .'

CHAPTER FIFTEEN
THE CHOICE

Before magic was outlawed in Camelot, Dragons had ruled the skies. But these mystical beasts had perished during the Great Purge alongside so many human sorcerers. Only one had survived, kept imprisoned by Uther as a symbol of his dominion over magic. This was the Great Dragon, the most powerful of them all.

But, in the vaults deep beneath Camelot, the Great Dragon was not cowed. Instead it had waited for the one it knew would come, the one whose arrival heralded the beginning of the end for Uther and his magic-free world. The warlock, Merlin. The Dragon had called Merlin and told the boy of his destiny, and since then Merlin had made his way down through the twisting turning tunnels into the darkness many times, asking the creature for advice and help.

Now a figure once again trod those paths – but it was not Merlin.

It was Gaius. And he had not been this way for many, many years.

He had not taken lightly the decision to venture beneath the palace. Once again, he was risking execution. But the choice he faced was so huge, and he had no one in whom he could confide.

The Dragon greeted him contemptuously. 'How old a man can become ... and yet change so little.'

'You have not changed either,' said Gaius, ignoring the taunt. 'But I'm not here for myself.'

'The boy.'

Gaius should have been surprised. But that one powerful magical being should know about another was perhaps not so unexpected. 'Merlin is in danger,' he said.

'No,' said the Dragon, 'it is my gaoler who stands in peril.'

This was at the very heart of Gaius' dilemma. 'Must Uther be sacrificed for the boy?'

'The time of Arthur and

MUST UTHER BE SACRIFICED FOR THE BOY?.

Merlin cannot come until Uther's is past,' replied the Dragon.

'But is that time now?'

'That is of your choosing . . .'

What sympathy could there be for Uther from this creature he had imprisoned – or from the orphan who had watched his parents burn? What sympathy could there be from either of them for the physician who had stood by the king's side throughout?

'I will not choose between them!' Gaius cried.

'Then turn a blind eye,' said the Dragon. 'That is, after all, your talent.'

And as the Dragon soared away, it left Gaius with his problem still unsolved – and his burden even heavier than before.

The next day Gaius stood before Uther. The summons had taken him by surprise, and he had been gripped with a terrible fear – had the king been told about Merlin? Had his own deception in shielding the boy been discovered?

Yet along with the terror there was a glimmer of relief. The choice would not be his after all.

But his first sight of Uther showed that his fears were unfounded: the king, although seeming ill at ease, was perfectly friendly.

Of course, this meant that Gaius' dilemma had not gone away, but it was soon swept from his mind by Uther's words. 'Gaius, you have been a loyal servant for many years. I look on you as a friend. You've been here since Arthur's birth and all that entailed.' He paused as Gaius nodded his understanding. 'What I'm trying to do, I think is best for you. I'll give you a generous allowance and make sure you are looked after.'

For a moment the doctor didn't understand what was meant, and then it sank in. 'You're retiring me?'

Uther stood up and paced around his throne, his awkwardness out of place in a man who was usually so sure and determined. 'I don't want you to worry. I'll allow you to continue living in your chambers until more suitable accommodation can be found.'

'Because I made one mistake. Although in truth, sire, it was not a mistake ... It was—'

'Yes, Gaius?' came a voice. Gaius never knew if he would really have told Uther the truth; if he would really have risked Merlin's life. Because at that moment a figure stepped out of the shadows – Edwin. And the words that Gaius had ready died in his throat.

'May I ask who is to be the next court physician?' he said instead, knowing the answer already.

The king was quick to dispel any idea of blame. 'None of this was Edwin's idea. Initially he turned down the offer. Surely you have no reason to oppose his appointment?'

For more than twenty years Gaius had wished for nothing but to serve his king. Everything he had done was to that end.

Everything. Even the things that Uther could never forgive – they'd all been done for him. How could Gaius stand aside now and not give the least warning of the revenge planned by this softly spoken traitor?

He opened his mouth to speak.

'If you have anything to say, then say it now, Gaius,' came that soft voice.

But Gaius could not say the words that would destroy the boy he cared for so much. If this was the time when he had to choose – then his choice was made. His choice was Merlin.

'This is difficult for both of us,' said

the king, who had no idea he'd just been condemned to death.

Gaius bowed sadly. 'I thank you for your patronage. It has been an honour and a pleasure to serve you and your family all these years.'

Unable to bring himself to meet Uther's eyes again, he left the chamber.

CHAPTER SIXTEEN
GOODBYES

Gaius was packing his belongings. He would not take up Uther's offer to remain in the palace: he could not bear to stand by and watch the things that were going to happen. He could not accept anything from the man he had betrayed.

Merlin came bursting through the door. It was clear from his face that he had already heard the news. 'Uther cannot do this to you!' he cried. 'I'll speak to Edwin – you can work together.'

'No!' If Gaius stayed, it would only jeopardize Merlin's safety. Edwin would always see him as a threat. 'Uther is right. It's time I stepped down. I cannot stay where there is no longer a use for me.'

'Then I'll come with you.' The boy's loyalty tore at Gaius' heart and he had to force himself to shake his head. How he wished he could accept the offer. But Camelot was where Merlin belonged; his destiny was with Arthur. Gaius must leave him, and he must leave him with no warning of what was to come. There was no doubt in the old doctor's mind that Edwin's threat to tell Uther about Merlin was real.

'Merlin, you're like a son to me. I never expected such a blessing so late in life.'

'And you are more than a father to me.'

The boy's words touched Gaius' heart, but made him even more determined.

'You must promise me that you will not waste your gifts,' he said, laying his hands on Merlin's shoulders.

'My gifts mean nothing without you to guide me.'

The physician smiled fondly. 'You have a great destiny. If I've had a small part to play in that, then I'm pleased.' He hoped Merlin would realize just how much he meant it. Gaius felt he had done very little in his life. There might have been times when he could have made a difference – but he had not taken those opportunities. If in helping Merlin he had achieved something at last, then he was glad.

'There is so much I've yet to learn. I need you to teach me,' said Merlin.

Gaius turned away. 'I'm afraid I am leaving here tonight. And there is nothing you can do or say that could persuade me otherwise.'

'I will not let this happen!' said Merlin firmly. He strode from the room; where he was going Gaius didn't know. To Uther,

perhaps, or Arthur, or even Edwin. It would make no difference. By the time the boy returned, Gaius would be gone.

'Goodbye, Merlin,' he whispered sadly.

GOODBYE, MERLIN.

It was Arthur whom Merlin had sought out. He liked to think that he and the prince were more than just master and servant; that there was a bond of friendship between them. He also liked to think that he could speak freely to the prince in a way that no other servant would have dared.

He suspected that Arthur did not view things in exactly the same way. Nevertheless the prince listened almost patiently to Merlin's passionate defence of Gaius.

Sadly for Merlin, however, Arthur did not agree with him. 'His mistake almost killed Morgana!' he said. 'And that wasn't his only one. Edwin said his work was riddled with errors.'

'That's nonsense,' said Merlin.

Arthur shrugged. 'No one wants Gaius to go, but my father's made his decision. There's nothing anyone can do.'

Merlin didn't want to give up, but he had to admit that Arthur was right about one thing. Once the king had made up his mind, he would never change it.

The king was happy with his decision. It was

a shame to see Gaius go, but things already seemed better with Edwin as court physician. He had spotted Uther's old battle wound, the shoulder that gave him so much pain, and had offered to provide a new prescription that he claimed would prove most effective. It was, he said, a remedy to cure all ills.

Uther looked forward to the time when he would feel his pain no more.

Gaius had hoped to avoid difficult good-byes. Just speaking to Merlin had hurt so much. But as he led his horse out to the gates of Camelot, Gwen ran up to him. 'You're leaving?' she asked.

Gaius nodded. 'Yes. I'm sorry I didn't come and say goodbye.'

'I don't want you to go,' she said. 'I don't trust Edwin. There was no blood in Morgana's ear – he did something to her, I know he did.'

Gaius looked swiftly over his shoulder, worried that her words might have been heard. 'You need to be careful who you say that to,' he told her.

She looked him straight in the eye. 'I'm saying it to you because you can do something about it.'

No! There was nothing he could do. 'I can't,' he said.

Gwen persisted. 'But you think the same, don't you? He's evil.'

'It's not that simple,' he said. And it wasn't. Edwin might have done evil deeds, might be planning to do more. But he had watched the parents he loved burn in a fire and had run in to save them. Uther had turned a child who loved into a child who hated, and although Gaius disliked the man that child had become, he also pitied him. He wished for Edwin's plans to be thwarted, yes – but was the man evil?

No, it certainly wasn't that simple.

'So you're going to turn your back on us,' said Gwen.

'I have no choice. I'm sorry.'

'In life you always have a choice.' Gaius had never heard the gentle girl speak so grimly before. 'Sometimes it's easier to think that you don't.'

'Well, then,' he told her with regret, 'my choice is to leave.'

The disappointment on her face hurt him, but he stood firm. He couldn't tell her what his choice really involved.

'Then I'll miss you,' she said. She leaned forward and kissed his cheek. 'Goodbye, Gaius.'

She walked off, and Gaius turned away sadly.

Yes, he had made his choice. And now he must live with it.

CHAPTER SEVENTEEN

A BATTLE OF MAGICKS

Edwin sat by the king's bedside. Uther had gratefully drunk the potion he'd provided. The remedy to cure all ills.

'My lord . . .' said Edwin quietly. And then, more forcefully, as the king did not respond, 'My lord!'

Uther's eyes opened, but he could barely focus.

'It seems the drugs I gave you have taken hold. Your body is now paralysed.' The king's eyelids drooped and Edwin quickly grabbed hold of his shoulders, shaking him back into consciousness. 'No! Open your eyes, my lord. I want my face to be the last face you ever see. You took my childhood from me, and now, finally, I take my parents' revenge.'

He opened his wooden box and brought out an unmoving black insect, placing it on Uther's pillow. 'Within a few hours the beetle will eat into your brain. And you will suffer as my parents suffered. And I long to hear you scream, as they screamed the night you gave the order for the fires to be lit.' He stood up, gazing down with hatred on his helpless victim. 'With your death, magic will return to Camelot.'

WITHIN A FEW HOURS THE BEETLE WILL EAT INTO YOUR BRAIN.

He began an incantation . . .

And Uther, as his mind drifted away, thought not of his pain, but the pain that would be in store for Camelot. He had dedicated more than two decades to protecting his beloved kingdom from the evils of magic, but now it would suffer and he felt such despair. Magic came with a friendly face, it brought offers of help, but these were mere masks that hid the horror beneath — as this wicked sorcerer was proving now. Within his mind, Uther begged Camelot for forgiveness, that he had finally failed it — that it would know the misery of magic again.

The spell finished and the beetle sprang to life. It headed towards the king's ear.

'Goodbye, Uther Pendragon,' said Edwin. Edwin entered his room. He placed his wooden box on the table and started to gather his possessions.

'I will not allow you to kill Uther.' Gaius stepped out of the shadows.

Edwin spun round. 'You've never had a problem letting people die before,' he said.

'Your parents were practising dark magic. Just like you.' Gaius approached the other man with some trepidation. Not because he was scared of Edwin; he was scared of what he had decided to do.

Edwin had offered him a choice – Uther's life or Merlin's. Gaius had chosen Merlin and believed that was the end of the matter.

But Gwen had believed he could – should – do something about Edwin, and that had made him reconsider. He realized that he was playing along with Edwin, remaining a pawn in the sorcerer's game. Merlin's life might be safe, but what of the boy's future? He would be in the charge of a murderer, of one who used magic for his own terrible ends. Gaius could not stand by and see Merlin corrupted, any more than he could stand by and watch him die.

Gaius thought he had made his decision, but he suddenly saw that the choice he had been offered was false. He did not have to choose between his king and the boy he loved like a son just because Edwin said so. There was a third option. One he shrank from, hardly able to believe he was considering it, but it had to be faced. Uther's life, Merlin's life — or Edwin's.

It might not come to that. He hoped it would not come to that. But Edwin must not be allowed to stay in Camelot. If nothing else, Gaius must frighten him, put him in fear for his life, make him back down, run away.

Gaius was an old man and Edwin was young and strong, despite the wounds he had suffered. More than that, Edwin was a powerful sorcerer.

But so had Gaius been, once.

'How do you propose to stop me?' Edwin asked, looking with disdain at the physician who stood before him.

And this was it – the moment of truth. Gaius began to intone words that had slept in his memory for many, many years.

 '*Wacie . . . wearglic . . .*' He pointed dramatically at Edwin.

Nothing happened.

'Hmm,' said Edwin. 'I think you meant: *Wacie eald.*' He raised a hand, and Gaius found himself flying through the air. He crumpled to the floor, momentarily stunned.

'You've forgotten everything, Gaius. You're getting too old. I have a cure, though.'

Gaius lay helplessly as Edwin cast another spell. A ring of flames sprang up around the old man, trapping him. They surged closer and closer. There was nothing he could do. Edwin was right. He had forgotten all the skills he once possessed. But it was not his own impending death that concerned him, it was the thought of his failure. The king would still die. And what would happen to Merlin . . . ?

Merlin! To Gaius' astonishment, he could hear Merlin's voice over the roar of the flames. He was somewhere outside the room, shouting. The words became clearer as he got nearer. 'Edwin! Arthur says Uther has Morgana's illness! You must come quickly!'

Edwin spun round as the door flew open. The astonished expression on Merlin's face might have been comical under other circumstances. 'What are you doing?' the boy cried.

'He was trying to kill the king. I couldn't let him,' said Gaius. He hated doing it. He had seen how happy Merlin had been when he thought he had an ally at last. The future had opened up to the boy, full of magic, and now it was crashing down around him.

Edwin stared Merlin straight in the eye. 'I can rule the kingdom now. With you at my side, we can be all-powerful.'

A life of magic. All that Merlin had ever wanted. But Gaius knew that he would never be tempted for a moment.

'Release him!' the boy shouted.

Edwin shrugged. 'Your loss, Merlin.' He gestured towards an axe that was hanging on the wall. It sprang off its supports and spun through the air towards the boy.

Gaius held his breath. But what he saw amazed him, for all that he had witnessed Merlin's skill before. No ordinary sorcerer could have cast a spell in time. No ordinary person could have got out of the way. But Merlin's eyes flashed gold and the axe slowed, as though spinning through treacle. It halted with its blade hanging over his head as Edwin cast more spells, urging it forward, urging it to kill him . . .

But Merlin was pushing it backwards. With a huge effort, he turned the axe so it

was facing the other way – and then he let go.

Edwin was still urging the axe to fly ... and it did.

He barely had time to scream.

CHAPTER EIGHTEEN

TO SAVE THE KING

With Edwin gone, the flames around Gaius died away, but for a few moments he was too shocked to move: shocked at what he'd witnessed, but even more shocked to find that both he and Merlin were still alive.

But what of Uther?

Merlin was frantically searching through Edwin's things. 'What are you doing?' Gaius asked.

The boy lifted a wooden box triumphantly.

'Edwin said he used these to cure Morgana. Maybe we can use them too.' He opened the lid, and Gaius looked on the contents in horror.

'Elanthia Beetles,' he breathed.

'Are they magical?' Merlin asked.

'Oh yes.' Suddenly everything was clear. He knew exactly how Morgana's illness had been caused. 'They can be enchanted to enter the brain and feed on it until they devour the person's very soul.' And this was happening to Uther right now. 'I must go to him!' Gaius exclaimed.

Together they ran to the king's chamber. But what could be done? None of Gaius' remedies had worked on Morgana; they would not work on Uther either. The only way to remove the beetle was by magic. But his battle with Edwin had shown that he was not up to the task. Uther's only hope was Merlin.

The boy was alarmed. 'We can't use magic on Uther – he'd kill us!'

'We don't have a choice.' In truth, there was always a choice. Gaius had learned that now. But he could not explain the whirling thoughts in his head; not now, not to Merlin.

If it was his risk to take, he would take it without hesitation. He had asked Merlin to step into danger before – although enchanting a weapon to kill the Griffin was not in the same league as performing magic on the king himself. He had just saved Merlin's life – how could he bear to put it at risk again so soon? But once again, this was not a choice between Merlin and Uther, however it might appear. There was a chance that both could be saved. 'There are times when it's necessary,' he told the boy.

'I don't know how!' Merlin protested.

Gaius turned to where the king lay – the

king he had tried to serve so faithfully. 'If you don't, he's going to die.'

Merlin looked at the doctor for a moment. Then he walked over to the bed and placed his hands over Uther's ears. He closed his eyes and began to chant a spell, nervously at first and then with more conviction. Then he withdrew his hands. In one palm lay a motionless beetle.

Gaius laughed with relief. 'Has anyone ever told you you're a genius!' he cried.

Merlin laughed too. 'Well, *you* certainly haven't.'

On the bed, the king began to wake.

'Do you remember them? His parents?' It was the next day. Uther was still weak, but recovering under Gaius' care. This was the first time the king had spoken of the man who had wanted him dead.

Gaius moved away so that Uther would not see his face as he answered. 'I remember them all, sire.'

'Gaius' – he turned back to the king – 'once again, you have saved my life. You have always served me well. And I know there are things I have asked you to do that you found difficult.'

'You have always done what you believe to be right,' the doctor answered.

He knew that was true. There were many things that Gaius did not like to think of, both in the past and the present. Many of the threats Uther faced were down to things that the king himself had done. Just in the last few months . . . a mother seeking revenge for her son's execution; the plots of a sorceress who, Gaius knew, had many, many reasons to hate the king, and now Edwin, whose life had been blighted by Uther's actions.

But through it all, the king had believed he was acting for the best. He believed that a world without magic was the right one for his people. Whatever he had done, he had done it for his kingdom.

And knowing that, Gaius remained loyal. Despite everything.

'I was not right to betray you,' the king said then. 'I'm sorry.' Uther apologizing was a rare thing indeed, and Gaius felt a rush of pleasure. But the king's next words shattered his composure. 'From now on, I will remember that in the fight against magic, you are the one person I can trust.'

FROM NOW ON, I WILL REMEMBER THAT IN THE FIGHT AGAINST MAGIC, YOU ARE THE ONE PERSON I CAN TRUST.

How many more times, Gaius wondered, would he have to break faith with the king in order to serve him? And how long would he be able to do so without Uther finding out . . . ?

The next day, all the great and the good of Camelot assembled in the council chambers. Uther smiled as he addressed the man who stood before his throne.

'I, my family and my kingdom are deeply indebted to you. And in honour of this, I not only reinstate you as court physician, but henceforth you are a freeman of Camelot.'

Gaius accepted the scroll the king offered him, the document that granted him the rights and privileges of his new status.

Uther clapped, as did Arthur and Morgana beside him. Merlin cheered, and Gwen's face was radiant. As he left the room on a sea of applause, Gaius felt quite overwhelmed – but very, very happy.

'Of course, it's all ridiculous,' he said to Merlin later. 'I didn't save Uther. *You* did.'

The boy laughed. 'For once I'm happy for someone else to take the credit.' And besides, it wasn't true. Merlin might have had the skills, but it was Gaius' actions and Gaius' knowledge that had saved the day. And even more than that ...

'You were prepared to sacrifice your life to save me.'

Gaius looked at him in astonishment. 'Where did you get that from?'

'I thought—' Merlin began, but the physician cut him off.

'Oh no, I didn't do anything. You saved me and you saved Uther.' He grinned. 'Maybe you *are* a genius!'

Merlin knew there was more to the tale than Gaius was telling, but he didn't press the matter. He was just relieved to have Gaius back again. How could he ever have considered that Edwin was a better physician? He would never be fooled by false heroics in future; his loyalties would remain with those who had earned them.

He knew that the real hero of the story was Gaius.

ALSO AVAILABLE

THE MAGIC BEGINS

Merlin arrives in Camelot full of excitement
and eager for adventure. But sorcery is
outlawed here and so he must learn
to hide his own magical talents.

When a mysterious new knight turns up
for the sword tournament, Merlin suspects
that dark magic is involved. He's determined
to investigate, but soon finds that keeping the
magic secret – and Prince Arthur alive –
is much harder than he thought . . .

978 0 553 82111 6

ALSO AVAILABLE

POTIONS AND POISON

A deadly plague is sweeping through
Camelot and Gwen is accused of witchcraft.

Somehow Merlin must find a cure and
save his friend from execution, but before
long Merlin finds his own life in danger!
Prince Arthur tries to help, but it seems
he may be walking into a trap . . .

978 0 553 82112 3

COMING SOON

SWORD AND SORCERY

When Merlin and Morgana join forces to
save a child the king has commanded be
put to death, they soon discover that going
against King Uther could prove fatal.

Meanwhile, a mysterious black knight arrives
to challenge the Knights of Camelot to
mortal combat. Old secrets, long hidden, are
stirring and the king is afraid for his only son.
The black knight seems invincible and Merlin
senses that only magic can stop him . . .

978 0 553 82502 2

ALSO AVAILABLE

MERLIN: THE COMPLETE GUIDE

Explore Merlin's world and find out all there is to know about the characters and their secrets. With facts and great imagery of all the cast, locations and props. Discover the lore and legend of Merlin!

Never seen before footage as well as maps and spells from the spell book finish this complete guide. It's a must have for any Merlin fan!

978 0 553 82108 6

ALSO AVAILABLE

MERLIN MYSTERY ACTIVITY BOOK

A mysterious stranger has taken Arthur
prisoner and Merlin has to find him and
set him free. Join Merlin on a dangerous
journey to save Arthur. Work through the
puzzles, play the games and answer the
riddles to help Merlin save his friend,
the future king of Camelot.

This activity book includes a free
spell notebook!

978 0 553 82105 5

ALSO AVAILABLE

MERLIN QUEST ACTIVITY BOOK

This Quest Activity book sets the stage for tournament day in Camelot. But danger lurks around every corner. An evil knight threatens Arthur, can he defeat him in battle? Join Arthur and his friends on their adventure around Camelot. Solve the puzzles, play the games and answer the riddles to help Arthur defeat the evil knight and win the tournament.

This activity book includes a free pull-out game!

978 0 553 82106 2

THE DRAGON'S CALL

When Merlin arrives in the great kingdom
of Camelot he discovers a dark side to the
bustling city: magic is outlawed on pain of
death! If he wants to stay alive, Merlin will
have to keep his unique magical talents a
closely guarded secret . . .

978 0 553 82109 3

VALIANT

A mysterious new knight arrives in Camelot
for the sword tournament. His fighting skills
are impressive but when an opponent is not
just injured but *poisoned*, Merlin suspects that
dark magic is involved. Merlin is determined
to expose the evil, but Arthur is next in line
to fight and time is running out . . .

978 0 553 82110 9

THE MARK OF NIMUEH

A deadly plague rages through
Camelot and it seems that sorcery is the
only explanation. When Gwen is arrested
for witchcraft, Merlin knows the wrong
person is accused, but can he uncover
the truth, find a cure and save his
friend from execution?

978 0 553 82114 7

THE POISONED
CHALICE

The sorceress Nimueh is weaving a
spell with powerful dark magic.
Her target is Merlin . . .

978 0 553 82115 4